Jake
in Trouble

Annette Butterworth

ILLUSTRATED BY
NICK BUTTERWORTH

ANDERSON'S PRIMARY SCHOOL

Hodder
Children's
Books

a division of Hodder Headline plc

l

Text copyright © Annette Butterworth 1997
Illustrations copyright © Nick Butterworth 1997

First published in Great Britain in 1997
by Hodder Children's Books
This paperback edition first published 1997

The right of Annette Butterworth to be identified
as the Author of the Work and the right of Nick Butterworth
to be identified as the Illustrator has been asserted by them in accordance
with the Copyright, Designs and Patents Act 1988.

10 9 8 7 6 5 4 3 2 1

A Catalogue record for this book is available from the British Library.

ISBN 0 340 69981 7

Printed and bound in Great Britain by
Mackays of Chatham PLC, Chatham, Kent

Hodder Children's Books
a division of Hodder Headline plc
338 Euston Road, London NW1 3BH

This
book is
dedicated to two
of my favourite people.
To Ben and Amanda,
with love.

Chapter One

Jake was excited. He was going on holiday to a farm.

Jake had never been on holiday before and he had never been to a farm.

He was looking forward to meeting all the animals. He knew there were sheep on the farm because he'd heard his owners, Mr and Mrs Foster, telling Sam.

Sam was Jake's favourite person. He lived in the house at the bottom of Jake's garden. Sam took Jake for walks in their local park. He always had a friendly word and pat for Jake. Jake usually stayed with Sam when the Fosters went on holiday. But this year, they were all going together.

Of course, Jake would miss his friends from the park, especially Holly, the collie, who lived next door. Jake told her how excited he was. He was especially looking forward to herding some sheep.

Holly didn't think he'd be allowed to do that. Farmers were very funny about their sheep. They were fussy about dogs. She'd even heard of a dog being shot at because he was in a field with sheep.

Jake found that hard to believe and thought Holly was just being silly. He was sure he'd be able to do it. Jake reminded Holly that his grandfather was a Belgian Shepherd dog, so he had sheep herding in his blood.

Holly looked doubtful. She said that

even though she was a Rough Collie, with lots of herding "in her blood", she wouldn't want to try and push big sheep about.

Jake wasn't worried. He was going to have a great time, and when he returned from holiday, he would tell her all about it.

Chapter Two

Jake was prepared for a long journey to the farm. He settled down in the back of the car.

He was right. It was a long way. He must have had eight sleeps! This was the longest journey he'd ever had and he was glad to jump out of the car into the farmyard.

The farmer's wife, Mrs Warden, greeted them and began to explain where the Fosters and Sam would find the caravans. Nobody noticed what Jake was doing.

He had spotted some farmyard ducks nesting in a corner, by a big barn. They were a different colour to the ducks in the park, but Jake was sure they'd be ready for a game.

He charged towards the ducks, expecting them to complain noisily at him, ruffle their feathers a bit and then settle back down onto their nests.

But these ducks didn't. They weren't used to boisterous dogs and they ran out of the farmyard, leaving their nests and their eggs to go cold.

Jake was surprised. The farmer's wife was very annoyed.

"I'm terribly sorry, Mrs Warden. He's used to chasing the ducks in the park." Mrs Foster said.

Mrs Warden looked at the eggs and

sighed. "Well, it can't be helped." she said. "He's had a long journey, so he's probably full of beans. But it might be best if you keep him on a lead around the farmyard. My husband doesn't like dogs who can't behave themselves."

At that moment, Mr Warden arrived in the farmyard with his sheepdog, who was called Shep.

Shep was a working sheepdog, and had herded sheep all his life. He was wary of town dogs. He thought they were stupid.

Eagerly, Jake ran to him, ready to introduce himself and make friends. But Shep walked straight past and ignored him.

Jake felt quite upset. He liked to be friends and he didn't care if his friends were clever or not, he liked them anyway. But this Shep seemed a very unfriendly dog.

The Fosters and Sam drove over to the field where their caravans were sited. There were only two so it was a peaceful spot. Jake was to stay in Sam's caravan because there would be more room.

The caravans were next to a field with sheep in. "That's good," thought Jake. "I'll probably get a chance to herd them. That'll show Shep I'm not completely stupid!"

Chapter Three

The next day started bright and early for the farm. Mr Warden was taking Shep to a local sheepdog trial. The sheepdogs would all compete against one another to see who was the best at herding sheep.

Everybody was very excited. Last year, they had come second, but this year Mr Warden was hoping to bring back the lovely silver cup awarded as first prize. He thought Shep was the best sheepdog he'd ever had.

Jake felt a bit jealous. He knew he had done a few useful things but it wasn't the same as working, like Shep.

The Fosters and Sam were invited along and they were all looking forward to it. Jake liked the look of the ham sandwiches they prepared for their picnic. He hoped he might get a bite of one later.

There was a short journey to the trial. It was being held in the grounds of a lovely old stately home. Mrs Foster was keen to look round it later, if possible.

When they arrived, the Fosters and Sam unpacked their chairs and picnic. They found themselves a good spot for watching the competition and settled down to enjoy the day.

Jake wasn't enjoying himself very

much at all. While other dogs seemed to be having a wonderful time, chasing sheep, he was tied up to Sam's deck chair.

"Oh well," he thought, "at least if I watch carefully, I might pick up a few tips. Then I can have a go myself."

This herding business looked easy. The sheep seemed a dull lot. The shepherd was doing a lot of whistling while the sheepdog raced up the field, collected a group of sheep and brought them back to the shepherd.

Jake wasn't impressed. He thought that by the end of the afternoon the sheep should know the way by themselves.

Some dogs were better than others. One unfortunate shepherd was herded into the pen with the sheep by his dog. He was squashed by the sheep against the side of the pen and another shepherd had to help him get out.

But the star of the day was Shep. Even
Jake had to admit that he did a superb
job. The sheep did exactly what they
should do and Mr Warden and Shep had
them in the sheep pen in record time.
Shep seemed really happy when he was
herding the sheep.

"I wish he was a bit friendlier," Jake
thought. "We could be good friends."

Mr Warden came over to speak to the
Fosters and Sam. Jake congratulated
Shep. But Shep stuck his nose in the air
and ignored him.

The results were read out. Mr Warden
and Shep had won easily. The beautiful

trophy, with the silver statue of a sheepdog on the top, was awarded to them, to keep for a year.

On the way back to the farm, Jake thought how nice it would be to prove to Shep that he wasn't the only one who could do useful things. Tomorrow, he would look for a chance to show that he could herd sheep as well.

"Nothing to it," thought Jake. "Easy."

Chapter Four

The next day, the Fosters and Sam decided to have a very early breakfast and then spend the day on a long walk. Jake was looking forward to it. He loved a good walk. There were lots of new smells here and there might even be some rabbits to chase.

The Fosters kept Jake on his lead as they walked through the farmyard. Shep, the collie, was lying down, waiting for the farmer to start work. He had a lot of sheep to move from one field to another and it was going to be a busy day. Jake said hello to him but Shep ignored him.

"I'm not talking to that idiot of a dog," thought Shep.

Jake was sad. "I'll show him," he thought.

Jake liked to lead the way when he was set free and once they had left the farmyard behind, Mrs Foster let him loose. The countryside was an ideal place for Jake to run in. It was an interesting walk, with mounds of rock to investigate and lots of trees to sniff at. The Fosters and Sam enjoyed the views and Sam spotted a rare bird that he'd never seen before. Jake was fed up because he had to sit still until the bird flew off.

They walked until midday when they stopped to eat their packed lunch. Jake had a drink of water and a dog biscuit. The Fosters and Sam were tired after their lunch and they all dozed off, lying in the sunshine.

Jake didn't think much of this. They were picnicking in a field with lots of interesting dips and lumps and bumps in it, so Jake decided to explore.

He discovered some exciting smells and found some fox's dung to roll in. Behind a gorse bush, he disturbed a rabbit. The rabbit rushed off and Jake chased after it. They ran round and round the field until the rabbit disappeared behind another bush.

Jake rushed over to follow it. Suddenly, he stopped. Danger. Jake could sense danger. It seemed as if the ground was not safe. It felt odd. It might even give way.

He stood still. He could feel the ground moving under his paws. He crouched low, and slowly turned round. He crawled back the way he had come until he felt the ground was safe again. He didn't like it at all and wondered what it was.

By now, the Fosters and Sam were waking up.

"Well, what do you think? Shall we go on or shall we head back?" said Mr Foster. They all agreed to go back to the farm.

For once, Jake wasn't sorry. He didn't want to stay in this field.

The party packed up and headed for home. They walked slower than in the morning and Jake was getting a bit impatient to be moving on.

They were quite close to the farm when Jake heard the farmer's sheep bleating in their new field. Jake was in front of the Fosters and Sam. He looked back at them, and then, without warning, he dashed off towards the field of sheep.

The Fosters were taken by surprise. They called Jake who seemed to have suddenly become deaf.

"I bet he's going after those sheep," said Mr Foster. "We'd better hurry up and catch him. Farmers can shoot at dogs that worry sheep."

They ran after Jake, but Jake had a big start on them, and he was much faster. He reached the field of sheep and looked for a hole in the fence. Finding a small one, he squeezed through it. The sheep ignored him and carried on grazing.

"Well, what now?" thought Jake. "I'll try to get them together in a group. That's what I need to do."

The sheep were scattered about the

field. He ran up to each sheep but they ignored him. One even chased him away.

"Right," thought Jake. "I know what will get them going," and he went up to a very big sheep and nipped its leg.

The sheep was furious. She rounded on Jake and chased him all over the field. The rest of the sheep started a huge commotion, cheering her on and barging each other out of the way.

Mr Warden heard the noise back at the farmhouse. He thought it must be a fox worrying his sheep. As he ran out of the farmhouse door, he was carrying his shotgun.

He ran up to the field. Jake heard a loud click. Then a bang. Jake was terrified. He fled to the fence and tried to find the hole. He couldn't. He started to panic. Frantically he ran up and down. Then something stung his ear. Jake whimpered. He'd been hit.

Another shot came whistling past his head.

The hole? Where was it?

Just as he had given up hope, there it was. At that moment, Mr Warden recognised Jake. He was livid. Sam and Mrs Foster came running up.

"Mr Warden, I'm terribly sorry. I don't know what's got into Jake. I'm so sorry," she said.

"Mrs Foster, you have to keep him away from my animals. He's a danger to them, and to himself." Mr Warden said. "I could have killed him."

Mrs Foster grabbed hold of Jake and yanked him by his collar. Jake thought she was going to strangle him.

Jake couldn't believe it – after all he had suffered, this was the treatment he was getting.

"You bad dog, Jake. You're lucky to be alive." Mrs Foster said.

Jake didn't feel very lucky at that moment.

Sam looked anxiously at him. He didn't agree with shooting. He felt Jake all over to check he had not been hurt.

Now Mr Foster had arrived. In his hurry to get to Jake, he had fallen badly and sprained his wrist. He was nursing his painful arm, and assured Mr Warden that Jake would get into no more trouble.

Back at the farmyard, Shep sneered at Jake. Herding sheep was a difficult job, needing expert dogs like him, not idiot town dogs like Jake. And then he turned his back on Jake and said no more to him.

Jake was thoroughly miserable. He'd been very frightened. He could have been killed. He was in disgrace, and he felt a failure. Far from being able to herd sheep, they had ignored him, then chased him and laughed at him. Shep had jeered at him and, worst of all, Mr Foster had sprained his wrist.

The Fosters and Sam returned to their caravans, and they all agreed that they would have to keep a very close eye on Jake. He mustn't be allowed to run around loose anymore, certainly not near the sheep.

Oh no! Jake knew that this would mean he would be tied up all the time.

After Sam had given him his supper, he disappeared under the bed and stayed there until the morning, sulking.

Chapter Five

The next day, the Fosters and Sam wanted to visit the museum in the local town.

There was, however, a problem with Jake. He couldn't go with them to the museum – dogs weren't allowed – and the caravan was too small to leave him in all day.

"I know," said Mrs Warden, "he can stay in the barn for the day. He can't come to any harm in there. It's very big and fairly empty at the moment. There's only old Rudi in there."

Mrs Warden was a kind-hearted lady and she felt sorry for Jake. She gave him a bone to chew on as he was led into the barn.

Rudi was a big, fat, old pig. She had been a very good pig for the Wardens, who spoilt her now. She was allowed the barn to herself. Being a mother was what she did best and she had produced lots of healthy piglets. Rudi beamed a great motherly smile at Jake and introduced herself.

Jake liked her straight away. She was the first friendly face he had found on the farm. He loved the smell of Rudi and the cosiness of her sty. She had her bed, made of straw, in one corner of the barn and she invited Jake over to the corner for a chat.

It wasn't long before the whole sorry tale of Jake's visit came out. Jake told her that he couldn't understand why the sheep wouldn't do as he wanted.

Rudi told him that sheep are really very stubborn. They only do what they want to do. They obeyed Shep because the farmer was there with him. Shep thinks he's in charge, but he's not.

Jake had to disagree with her. He thought Shep definitely knew what he was doing with sheep.

Jake asked Rudi if she had any idea why Shep was so horrible to him. Rudi told him that Shep was a very proud dog and he had no close friends, even on the farm. He didn't think anybody was as clever as him and he was rather a lonely dog.

Rudi said that Shep was very wary of strangers. But she was sure that he would like Jake as a friend. She could tell Jake was a lively dog who enjoyed himself. Shep always concentrated on only one thing, which meant he couldn't sense danger and was easily taken by surprise. He wouldn't be any good in a town. Rudi was sure Jake could teach Shep a thing or two, even if it wasn't how to herd sheep!

Jake was sure Shep would never listen to a word he said.

Jake chatted about all his town friends, how together they had saved their local park. He was very modest. He didn't tell Rudi that he was the one that had saved it. He told her about his visit to Crufts Dog Show and how wonderful it was.

And he talked about Sam, his friend, who was always on his side. He told her about their football games together every day, in the local park. Jake loved football and he was very good at it. He chatted about Holly and how much he missed his friends from the park.

This made him even more sad and he slumped down on the floor, his ears down, feeling very low.

Rudi tried to cheer Jake up. She wondered if he would like some of her potato peelings. Of all the leftovers given to her each day, she saved the peelings to eat as a special treat. But Jake could have them today. Rudi believed that most problems could be solved by something tasty to eat.

Jake looked at them. He usually had a huge appetite but even he drew the line at raw potato peelings.

He appreciated the thought, but politely turned down the offer. Rudi didn't need much persuasion and ate the peelings whilst trying to cheer Jake up. She was sure that Shep would change his mind about Jake. Jake was obviously a very clever dog.

Jake appreciated Rudi's efforts. He was glad to have found at least one friend on the farm. But he didn't think Shep would ever change his mind.

Chapter Six

Sam was worried about Jake. He thought Jake was missing his pals, and of course, he was right.

Sam wanted to cheer Jake up. He usually played football with him, but since the shooting, he didn't think it was safe to let him off the lead around the farm.

Sam remembered that he had seen a big park nearby. He asked the Fosters if he could take Jake there.

"That would be lovely, Sam. Why don't you borrow the car and drive there?" Mrs Foster said. "Do you mind if we stay here? I think John needs to rest. His wrist is very swollen."

"That's fine. And we don't need the car, thank you. Jake and I can walk there," Sam replied.

Jake was very pleased to be going somewhere just with Sam, especially as Sam had the football bag in his hand. Trotting along the country lanes at Sam's side, he thought perhaps things weren't so bad after all.

As they approached the park, Sam was surprised to see so many people. A big banner was stretched across the entrance, saying "Country Fair".

A large arena had been set up. In the centre, there was a big circle with a stage in the middle and seats all around it. The rest of the arena was filled with stalls selling all kinds of goods: cheeses, jams, cakes, sausages, baskets, candles, leather goods. Jake thought he could see some chocolates. He hoped they could visit the stalls after their game.

Sam and Jake had a long and lively game of football. Jake felt like he'd been let out of prison. He threw himself at the football. He headed the ball eight times on the trot, which was a record for him.

"Bet Shep can't do this!" he thought.

After their game, Jake and Sam returned to the Country Fair. It was very busy.

There were crowds of people bustling around the stalls. Jake was disappointed to see that the chocolate stall was very busy and nearly all the chocolates had been sold. He did manage to eat a sample piece of cheese that had fallen off the cheese stall and he thought it was very nice.

When they reached the arena, Sam spotted a spare seat near the front, so he sat down to watch.

A group of men came into the arena. Jake had never seen anyone dressed like them before. They had ribbons all over them, even on their feet, and some jingling brass bells tied to their shoes. They were carrying big thick sticks which also had ribbons tied to them. To Jake's amazement, they started running round the circle, ringing their bells and bashing their sticks together.

Jake didn't like the sticks. They looked like they could really hurt. He started to growl.

"It's alright, boy," Sam said. "They're only Morris dancers."

At that moment, the men came close to Sam and nearly hit him. This was too much for Jake. He jumped up and rushed into the middle of them, trying to get their sticks, barking loudly. The Morris dancers tried to catch him, so they could finish their dance. Unfortunately, one of the Morris Men got tangled up in his own ribbons and fell over. His stick fell from his hand. Jake grabbed hold of it and rushed over to Sam.

Sam took Jake by the collar and retrieved the stick. As he gave it back to the Morris Man he said how sorry he was.

But the Morris Men were not cross at all.
They were laughing heartily. In fact, they
thought Jake had added something to
their performance. He had certainly
livened things up. The audience loved it
too. They thought Jake was a part of the
act.

Sam decided to take Jake back to the
farm quickly, before he could get into
any more mischief. He was very relieved
that the Morris dancers had been so nice.

As Sam and Jake arrived at the farmyard, Mr Warden was standing at the farmhouse door, looking very worried.

"What's wrong?" asked Sam.

"It's Shep," replied Mr Warden, "he's gone missing. This morning, I was getting ready to check on the sheep. I whistled for Shep, but he didn't come. He is not on the farm. It's not like Shep to stray, he can always find his way back. We've looked everywhere on the farm and now I'm wondering if he's been stolen. He's a prize-winning sheepdog, and there's lots of folks would want him."

"Perhaps you should search further afield," suggested Sam.

"We'll have to." replied Mr Warden, "But it's not like Shep to leave the farm."

Sam returned to the caravans and told the Fosters. "They're going to organise a search party to look for him," he said.

"He's probably been stolen," thought Jake. "Now, if I could only find him, and the thief. They wouldn't call me a useless town dog then."

But Jake didn't get a chance to look. The next day, he watched the search party set out.

He stayed tied up outside the caravan. Lots of people turned out. Shep was well known, and Mr Warden had offered a generous reward.

Jake heard Mr Warden tell the people where they were going to search. They would look tomorrow as well if they had to.

"I wish I could go with them," Jake thought. But, since the shooting, the Fosters and Sam hadn't let Jake out of their sight.

Much later, the search party returned, with still no sign of Shep. It began to look as if he had been stolen.

Chapter Seven

The next morning, the search party set off again to look for Shep. By the afternoon, they had still not returned, and nor had Shep.

The Fosters and Sam were preparing their evening meal. They were all inside the Fosters' caravan. Jake was tied to a post outside. His lead was looped over the top. He started to chew at it, then he pulled at it, but it was a very strong lead and he couldn't break it.

Then Jake had an idea. Slowly, he started to push the lead up the post.

It was nearly at the top when Sam came out of the caravan to peel some potatoes in the sunshine. Jake sat still immediately and hoped that Sam didn't notice the lead was nearly at the top of the post. Eventually Sam went back into the caravan and Jake carried on pushing the lead until it reached the top of the post. Then, it slipped off. Jake was free.

He ran off with the lead trailing behind him.

Some time later, when Sam and the Fosters had finished eating, they noticed Jake had gone. They were frantic. Jake would get himself killed this time. They called and called but he was already a long way away.

Jake didn't have any plan of how to find Shep. He wanted to find a clue or a fresh smell that might help him. He ran for a long time, to make sure the Fosters wouldn't follow him. Then he realised he was getting near the field that he didn't like, the field where he had sensed danger.

Jake stopped quickly. He wasn't going to risk that field.

Then he smelt something. It was not a smell that people would recognise, but one that animals know well. Fear. It was the smell of something, or someone, who is afraid. Carefully, Jake crawled into the field and the smell got stronger. The closer Jake got to danger, the stronger the smell was getting.

Then Jake knew what he could smell. He could smell Shep. And Shep was frightened. But Jake couldn't see him anywhere.

What should he do? He could sense great danger all around him.

He should turn back.

But Jake couldn't turn back. Shep needed his help, wherever he was. And Jake bravely carried on, crawling through the field.

Just as the smell was at its strongest, and the danger felt unbearable, Jake saw it. The ground had fallen away right in front of him and there was a small hole, just big enough for a dog to fall through.

Jake listened. He could hear something faint but unmistakable. It was the sound of a dog whimpering.

When he dared to look down the hole, it was very dark. Eventually, his eyes got used to it and then he could see that the hole was very deep. As he looked, he thought he could see a little shape on a narrow ledge halfway down.

He called. The little shape moved and howled back at him.

It was
Shep! He
was so
pleased to
see Jake.
He had been
so stupid. He'd
raced after a rabbit and ended up falling
down here.

Shep's pleasure at seeing Jake high above him soon faded when he realised that Jake couldn't get him out. Shep had hurt his leg badly and he couldn't move from the little ledge. He would fall further down the deep hole. He had no food but luckily, there was water dripping past him and he could drink that.

But both dogs realised that unless Jake could get help, Shep wasn't going to survive.

Jake didn't know what he was going to do. He wasn't allowed to be off the lead around the farm, and after this, he would be watched even more closely.

Shep went very quiet. Jake reassured him that he would do whatever he could to get him rescued. Jake would find a way. He must.

The Fosters were furious with Jake when he returned to the farm.

"We'll have to keep him shut up most of the time now," Mr Foster said.

"At least he's come back," Sam said. He was very pleased to see Jake.

Jake prowled up and down. He was very restless and he wouldn't eat his food. He couldn't sit still and kept pulling at Sam's clothes and crying at the door.

He couldn't make them understand.

Jake was really worried. He didn't mind for himself. He didn't mind so much if he was kept shut up, especially if he had Rudi for company.

But he was very worried for Shep. He knew that if he didn't get help very soon, Shep wouldn't last out much longer on that little ledge.

Chapter Eight

The next day, the Fosters and Sam needed to buy some food. So Jake was left in the barn, with Rudi. Jake hurriedly told her all about Shep.

Rudi was pleased Jake had found Shep. She said how clever he'd been.

Jake didn't feel very clever. He couldn't think of a way to rescue Shep. There was no point being clever enough to find him, without being able to rescue him.

Rudi knew that the search party was

going out for the last time, today. She thought that Jake should try and get them to follow him, so he could lead them to Shep. They'd try to catch Jake at least, wouldn't they, after all the fuss with the sheep.

Jake needed to find a way out of the barn, which seemed impossible.

He looked at the big door. It was bolted on the outside. No way of opening that. He noticed that the door handle was like the one on the back door at home. He could let himself in at home by jumping up and pulling the handle down. The barn door opened outwards, so if it didn't have a bolt on the outside, Jake was sure he could just pull down the handle and push the door open.

But there was a bolt, and even as Jake told Rudi, he knew it was no good.

Then Rudi had an idea. Dear old

Rudi, who usually only worried about her next meal. But it was thinking about her breakfast that gave Rudi her idea.

Rudi whispered her plan to Jake. Mrs Warden would be along soon, with Rudi's breakfast, leftovers from the farm. She would have to unbolt the door to get into the barn. She would shut it behind her but, if Jake was quick, he could open the door and rush away before she noticed. Rudi would do her best to distract her and give Jake more time.

Jake thought it was a brilliant plan. Rudi blushed.

Mrs Warden arrived with the breakfast. At that moment, Rudi began to moan, as if she had stomach pains.

"What is it, old girl? Not feeling yourself this morning? Perhaps I'd better not give you this," Mrs Warden said.

Rudi stopped groaning straight away.

She wanted to help, but she also wanted her breakfast.

But this gave Jake just enough time and while Mrs Warden wasn't looking, he leaped up at the door, pulled down the handle and ran out of the barn into the farmyard.

The search party was just preparing to leave. Jake rushed around them, barking loudly to get their attention.

When Mr Warden realised who it was, he shouted, "Quickly, catch him quickly!

He'll get himself lost next. Get that dog back in the barn."

Jake ran backwards and forwards. He wanted people to follow him, but he couldn't let them catch him. It was very tricky and it took all his skill to weave in and out without being caught.

The farmyard was in uproar. Geese and ducks were flapping all over the place. People were falling over them and one another as they tried to catch Jake.

Jake's idea was to lead them out of the farmyard. They followed him a little way but then they gave up.

This was no good at all. This was not what Jake had in mind. He'd escaped from the barn but he couldn't get the search party to follow him. Everything had gone wrong. What could he do?

Jake decided that at least he could check if Shep was still alive.

When he came to the field, he crawled carefully to the hole and looked down to see Shep, still stuck on the little ledge. Shep was very pleased to see Jake again but he was disappointed that Jake hadn't managed to get the rescuers to follow him.

Jake chatted for a long time to Shep, trying to cheer him up. Shep was feeling very cold and damp, and extremely hungry. He was beginning to give up hope of being rescued.

As he lay carefully at the top of the hole, Jake suddenly caught sight of something glinting. It was a little way down, and Jake had to be very careful as he tried to see what it was.

Then Jake recognised it. It was a small metal disc, like he and all his friends had attached to their collars. Jake realised he was looking at Shep's name tag. It had

come off his collar as
he had fallen.

Then Jake had
an idea.

Carefully, Jake
pressed himself as

flat as he could against the earth and
slowly leaned forward.

It was very scary. Jake found himself
looking down into the big black hole.
One sudden movement and he would
find himself down there with Shep, or
perhaps falling past him into the
blackness.

Slowly, he reached forward and
grabbed the metal disc in his mouth. But,
as he did, the earth started to crumble
away beneath him. He stopped dead. He
was perched at the top of the hole, with
the disc in his mouth.

He couldn't move. When he tried to

make the smallest movement, the earth started to fall into the hole again, threatening to take him with it.

He stayed still for a very long time. He didn't dare shout down to Shep.

After what seemed like ages, Jake knew he had to risk moving. He couldn't stay there.

Slowly, little by little, he moved first one part of his leg, then another, back from the mouth of the hole. Beneath him, lumps of mud and stones fell into the mine. He had to force himself to be patient and move very slowly, something he wasn't used to doing.

At long last, he managed to reach safer ground, away from the mouth of the hole. Excitedly, he shouted down to Shep, to tell him he'd managed to get his name tag. Jake explained his plan.

Shep was full of admiration. Jake was

so brave and rather clever. His cleverness was different to Shep's and Shep had to admit there were things Jake could do that he couldn't. Thank goodness!

Jake said goodbye and raced off towards the farm.

Chapter Nine

When Jake got back to the farmyard, the search party had returned and they all looked very sad.

They sat in a circle, drinking tea with the farmer, who thanked them for all their efforts.

"We've tried very hard," Mr Warden said, "but sadly, I have to say, that we'll never see Shep again."

At that moment, Jake rushed into the

middle of the circle. In his enthusiasm, he jumped on top of Mr Warden and nearly knocked him off the straw bale he was sitting on.

"Oh, not you!" Mr Warden said, "Now why couldn't you get lost?"

Then Jake dropped Shep's name tag into Mr Warden's lap and danced around excitedly.

"Mad, completely mad, you are," Mr Warden said.

Then Mrs Warden noticed the tag. "What's that in your lap?" she asked. "What has Jake just dropped?"

Mr Warden picked up the tag and looked at it carefully. Then his face lit up.

"It's Shep's name tag! How did you find it, boy?" he said to Jake.

Jake barked loudly and started to run out of the farmyard. He ran back to Mr

Warden and started to push him with his nose.

"Alright, boy, I get the message," laughed Mr Warden. "You want us to follow you."

At last he had made them understand! Jake rushed out of the farmyard with the rescuers close behind.

When they reached the field, Jake slowed down and started to crawl forward. Jake was very nervous. He didn't want to go back to the hole. The earth around it was ready to collapse.

Mr Warden could see that Jake thought the field was dangerous so he stopped everybody.

"I think I'd better follow Jake alone. It looks like he thinks the ground isn't safe." Mr Warden copied Jake, following him carefully across the field.

Eventually they came to the hole and Jake stopped. He knew that they shouldn't go any nearer.

He barked loudly to let Shep know he'd arrived and that Mr Warden was with him.

Shep barked back, and Mr Warden heard him. "Well, well. It's an old mine shaft. I didn't know this was here. And that's Shep's bark. He must be trapped down there. Oh well done Jake, you clever boy. I have misjudged you. You found Shep and you were clever enough not to fall down yourself."

Mr Warden crept forward to the edge of the hole. He looked down and once his eyes had got used to the gloom, he could see where Shep was stuck.

"Alright, Shep old boy. We'll soon have you out of there."

Shep barked weakly to Mr Warden.

Mr Warden called for two rescuers to help him. They had ropes and equipment, so they could go down the deep hole.

Firstly, they did what they could to make the top safer with some pieces of wood. Then one of them was lowered down into the hole. He made a sling out of Mr Warden's jacket and carefully put Shep inside it. Slowly Shep was pulled up out of the hole.

Shep was pleased to see everybody but he was most pleased to see Jake. He nuzzled at Jake and licked his face, thanking him for rescuing him. He was so sorry that he had been unfriendly.

Jake told him to not to worry. They could be good friends now.

Carefully, Jake and the rescuers carrying  Shep, crept out of the field.

They returned to the farm to be met by the Fosters and Sam, who couldn't find Jake in the barn and were worried about what had happened.

They were very relieved to see Jake with Mr Warden and thrilled when the farmer explained how Jake had led them to Shep.

"You've got a grand dog there, Mr Foster." Mr Warden said. "When I first met him, I thought he'd be nothing but trouble. Shows how wrong you can be!"

Mr and Mrs Warden were thrilled to have Shep back. To show their gratitude to Jake they offered the reward money to the Fosters and another week's holiday on the farm. The Fosters and Sam were pleased to accept the extra week but didn't accept the money. Jake had found Shep and money didn't mean anything to Jake. He was just pleased that, at last, Shep was his friend.

Shep had to hop about. He had hurt his leg badly but he was determined to make sure Jake enjoyed the rest of his holiday.

He offered to teach Jake to herd sheep. At first Jake thought this would be very nice. Then he looked across at the big sheep grazing in the field. He thanked Shep very much, but he thought perhaps he'd better leave it to the experts.

Jake had had a lovely holiday. He'd found a new friend in Shep and even made friends with Mr Warden.

Now he was looking forward to going home and telling Holly about his holiday. He would tell her about the rescue. He'd tell her about the Morris Men. He'd tell her about Shep and Rudi the pig.

He would tell Holly all about his adventures. Well, perhaps not quite all.

He might leave out the bit about the sheep